NICKI WEISS

Where Does the Brown Bear Go?

A TRUMPET CLUB SPECIAL EDITION

ISBN 0-590-16330-2

12 11 10 9 8 7 6 5 4 3 2   6 7 8 9/9 0 1/0

Printed in the U.S.A.

Set in Weidemann Medium

FOR JOHNNY

AND STEVIE

When the lights go down
On the city street,
Where does the white cat go, honey?
Where does the white cat go?

When evening settles
On the jungle heat,
Where does the monkey go, honey?
Where does the monkey go?

They are on their way.

They are on their way home.

When shadows fall
Across the dune,
Where does the camel go, honey?
Where does the camel go?

When the junkyard is lit
By the light of the moon,
Where does the stray dog go, honey?
Where does the stray dog go?

They are on their way.

They are on their way home.

When the sun sinks far
Behind the seas,
Where does the seagull go, honey?
Where does the seagull go?

When night in the forest
Disguises the trees,
Where does the brown bear go, honey?
Where does the brown bear go?

They are on their way.

They are on their way home.

The stars are bright and a warm wind blows
Through the window tonight, honey,
Through the window tonight....

And everyone is home.